The Puffin Book of Five-minute Stories

This book belongs to

....

The Puffin Book of Five-minute Stories

Illustrated by Steve Cox

PUFFIN BOOKS

PUFFIN BOOKS

Published by the Penguin Group
Penguin Books Ltd, 27 Wrights Lane, London W8 5TZ, England
Penguin Putnam Inc., 375 Hudson Street, New York, New York 10014, USA
Penguin Books Australia Ltd, Ringwood, Victoria, Australia
Penguin Books Canada Ltd, 10 Alcorn Avenue, Toronto, Ontario, Canada M4V 3B2
Penguin Books (NZ) Ltd, 182–190 Wairau Road, Auckland 10, New Zealand

Penguin Books Ltd, Registered Offices: Harmondsworth, Middlesex, England

First published 1998
1 3 5 7 9 10 8 6 4 2

This edition copyright © Penguin Books Ltd, 1998
The acknowledgements on page 124 constitute an extension to this copyright page
Illustrations copyright © Steve Cox, 1998
All rights reserved

Filmset in 17 on 25pt Garamond 3

Made and printed in Italy by L.E.G.O.

British Library Cataloguing in Publication Data
A CIP catalogue record for this book is available from the British Library

ISBN 0–670–87680–1

CONTENTS

THE LITTLE WOODEN HORSE

from

ADVENTURES OF THE
LITTLE WOODEN HORSE

Ursula Moray Williams

ONE DAY UNCLE PEDER made a little wooden horse. This was not at all an extraordinary thing, for Uncle Peder made toys every day of his life, but oh, this was such a brave little horse, so gay and splendid on his four green wheels, so proud and dashing with his red saddle and blue stripes! Uncle Peder had never made so fine a little horse before.

'I shall ask five shillings for this little wooden horse!' he cried.

What was his surprise when he saw large tears trickling down the newly painted face of the little wooden horse.

'Don't do that!' said Uncle Peder. 'Your paint will run. And what is there to cry about? Do you want more spots on your sides? Do you wish for bigger wheels? Do you creak? Are you stiff? Aren't your stripes broad enough? Upon my word I can see nothing to cry about! I shall certainly sell you for five shillings!'

But the tears still ran down the newly painted cheeks of the little wooden horse, till at last Uncle Peder lost patience. He picked him up and threw him on the pile of wooden toys he meant to sell in the morning. The little wooden horse said nothing at all, but went on crying. When night came and the toys slept in the sack under Uncle Peder's chair the tears were still running down the cheeks of the little wooden horse.

In the morning Uncle Peder picked up the sack and set out to sell his toys.

At every village he came to the children ran out to meet him, crying 'Here's Uncle Peder! Here's Uncle Peder come to sell his wooden toys!'

Then out of the cottages came the mothers and the fathers, the grandpas and the grandmas, the uncles and the aunts, the elder cousins and the godparents, to see what Uncle Peder had to sell.

The children who had birthdays were very fortunate: they had the best toys given to them, and could choose what they would like to have. The children who had been good in school were lucky, too. Their godparents bought them wooden pencil-boxes and rulers and paper-cutters, like grown-up people. The little ones had puppets, dolls, marionettes and tops. Uncle Peder had made them all, painting the dolls in red and yellow, the tops in blue, scarlet and green. When the children had finished choosing, their mothers, fathers, grandpas, grandmas, uncles, aunts, elder cousins and god-parents sent them home, saying, 'Now let's hear no more of you for another year!' Then they stayed behind to gossip with old Peder, who brought them news from the other villages he had passed by on his way.

Nobody bought the little wooden horse, for nobody had five shillings to spend. The fathers and the mothers, the grandpas and the grandmas, the uncles and the aunts, the elder cousins and the godparents, all shook their heads, saying, 'Five shillings! Well, that's too much! Won't you take any less, Uncle Peder?' But Uncle Peder would not take a penny less.

'You see, I have never made such a fine little horse before,' he said.

All the while the tears ran down the nose of the little wooden horse, who looked very sad indeed, so that when Uncle Peder was alone once more he asked him, 'Tell me, my little wooden horse, what is there to cry about? Have I driven the nails crookedly into your legs? Don't you like your nice green wheels and your bright blue stripes? What is there to cry about, I'd like to know?'

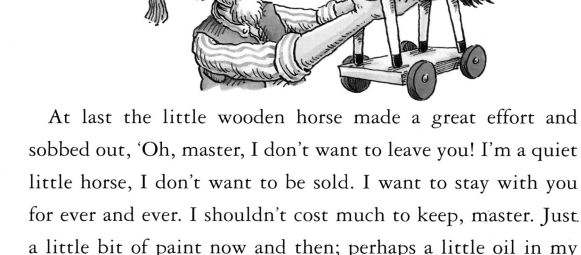

At last the little wooden horse made a great effort and sobbed out, 'Oh, master, I don't want to leave you! I'm a quiet little horse, I don't want to be sold. I want to stay with you for ever and ever. I shouldn't cost much to keep, master. Just a little bit of paint now and then; perhaps a little oil in my wheels once a year. I'll serve you faithfully, master, if only you won't sell me for five shillings. I'm a quiet little horse, I am, and the thought of going out into the wide world breaks my heart. Let me stay with you here, master – oh, do!'

Uncle Peder scratched his head as he looked in surprise at his little wooden horse.

'Well,' he said, 'that's a funny thing to cry about! Most of my toys want to go out into the wide world. Still, as nobody wants to give five shillings for you, and you have such a melancholy expression, you can stop with me for the present, and maybe I won't get rid of you after all.'

When Uncle Peder said this the little wooden horse stopped crying at once, and galloped three times round in a circle.

'Why, you're a gay fellow after all!' said Uncle Peder, as the little wooden horse kicked his legs in the air, so that the four green wheels spun round and round.

'Who would have thought it?' said Uncle Peder.

CLEVER CAKES

Michael Rosen

Once there was a girl called Masha who lived with her granny at the edge of the woods.

One day Masha said, 'Granny, can I play outside with my friends?'

'Yes, Masha,' said Granny, 'but don't wander off into the woods, will you? There are dangerous animals there that bite . . .'

Off went Masha to play with her friends. They played hide-and-seek. Masha went away to hide and she hid right deep in the woods. Then she waited for her friends to find her. She waited and waited but they never came. So Masha came out of her hiding place and started to walk home. She walked this way, then that way, but very soon she knew she was lost.

'He-e-e-lp!' she shouted. 'He-e-e-e-lp!'

But no one came.

Then very suddenly up came a massive muscly bear.

'Ah hah!' said the bear. 'You come with me, little girl. I'm taking you home. I want you to cook my dinner, wash my trousers and scrub the floor in my house.'

'I don't want to do that or anything like it, thank you very much,' said Masha. 'I want to go home.'

'Oh no you don't,' said the bear. 'You're coming home with me.' And he picked up Masha in his massive muscly paws and took her off to his house.

So now Masha had to cook and clean and wash and dust all day long. And she hated it. And she hated the massive muscly bear. So she made a plan.

She cooked some cakes, and then she said to the bear, 'Mr Bear, do you think I could take some cakes to my granny?'

I'm not falling for a stupid trick like that, thought the bear. If I let her go to her granny's, she'll never come back.

'No you can't,' he said. 'I'll take your cakes to her myself.'

And he thought, I'll eat all those cakes. Yum, yum, and yum again.

'Right,' said Masha, 'I'll put the cakes in this basket. Don't eat them on the way to Granny's, will you? Cos if you do, something terrible will happen to you.'

'Of course I won't eat the cakes,' said the bear.

As soon as the bear's back was turned, Masha jumped into the basket. When he turned round, he picked up the basket and walked off.

After a while, the bear got tired – ooh, that basket was so heavy, it was pulling off his arm – so he sat down.

'Now for the cakes,' he said.

But Masha called out from inside the basket, 'Don't you eat us, Mr Bear. We're little cakes for Masha's granny.'

You should have seen that bear jump!

'The cakes heard me. Oh, yes, Masha did say if I ate them something terrible would happen to me. I'd better leave them alone.'

So up got the bear and walked on . . . and on . . . and on . . . until he began to feel hungry. He thought, if I could eat the cakes without them knowing, surely nothing terrible will happen to me. But how can I eat them without them knowing? Then he said out loud, 'Oooh, I wonder if those little cakes would like to hop out of the basket and come for a walk with me.'

But Masha called out from inside the basket, 'Don't you dare touch us, you great greedy glut. We're little cakes for

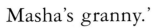

Masha's granny.'

The bear nearly jumped out of his jacket.

'Woo-hoo, those devilish little cakes knew that was a trick. What clever cakes. Next time I won't say anything at all. I'll just sit down and gobble them up. Yum, yum, and yum again.'

So up he got and walked on . . . and on . . . and on . . .

But now the bear was getting really very, very hungry. It felt like there was a huge hole in his belly. This time he remembered not to speak. Very carefully he sat down, and slo-o-o-o-wly he reached out his massive muscly paw for the basket. But Masha, peeking through the holes in the basket, could see what the bear was up to and she called out, 'Don't you dare touch us, you horrible great greedy glut. We're little cakes for Masha's granny and if you touch us, we'll jump out of the basket faster than you can blink, and we'll eat you up, ears and all.'

'Zoo-wow, those cakes must be magic!' said the bear. 'I'd be crazy to touch them. I'd better take them to Masha's granny as quickly as I can or something terrible will happen to me.' And he hurried on to Granny's house.

When he got there he shouted, 'Open the door, Granny!'

Granny came to the door and when she saw a great big bear standing there she was scared stiff.

But little Masha called out from the basket, 'Look out, Bear, your time's up. Now we're going to eat you.'

The bear dropped the basket, turned, and ran off shouting, 'Help, help, the cakes are going to eat me, the cakes are going to eat me!'

As soon as the bear was off and away, out of the basket popped Masha. Oh, how pleased Granny was to see her, and how pleased Masha was to see her granny! They hugged and kissed each other so many times that there were no kisses left till the next day.

'What a clever girl you are to trick that big bear,' said Granny.

'Never mind that,' said Masha. 'Let's get these cakes inside us.'

And that's what they did. Yum, yum, and yum again!

THE ORCHESTRA THAT LOST ITS VOICE

Geraldine McCaughrean

IN THE HEART of a large city, in a round building, in a room with chandeliers and a thousand folding red seats, a famous orchestra plays every night.

Boom-boom-boom-BOOM!

Sometimes it plays music by Strauss: *Dum-dum-dum-DUM!* And sometimes it is by Glenn Miller: *Da-dididdy-daa-aa-diddy!* But most often, it was by Beethoven: *Boom-boom-boom-BOOM!*

The musicians of the Royal Symphonic have been playing in the concert hall since they were young, and most of them are old now, with thinning hair and knobbly fingers. But every evening they play, and every night they pack away their instruments in the big cupboard under the stage. It is dark and quiet, though sometimes the great double bass snores, and the flute talks in her sleep.

But it was very different on the night of the storm! Shortly after midnight, the orchestra was woken by tinkling, rattling and banging.

'There's another orchestra out there!' cried the snare drum. 'I can hear banging!'

The triangle chimed in, 'And I can hear another triangle!'

'Other instruments are doing our job!' screamed the first violin.

'We'll soon see about *that*!' said the kettle-drum.

He rolled his great weight against the doors of the cupboard, and they burst open with a splintering of wood. The

tambourine rolled over to the wall switches, and the concert hall was flooded with light.

But there *was* no other orchestra. There was not an instrument in sight. The concert hall was playing a music of its own.

The windows were rattling in their frames, while raindrops plinked on the glass. The chandeliers trembled, and the great doors at the back of the hall banged with every gust of wind. A draught as sharp and icy as a note on a piccolo whipped along the corridor and under the seats. The radiators were off, so it was very cold. And, worst of all, a skylight had been left open and rain was driving through on to the unhappy instruments below.

Shivering with horror and cold, they turned back to cower in their cupboard. But they could not close the doors again, and all night long cold draughts fretted round them.

Next day, the audience began to arrive as usual. The conductor whispered to his musicians, 'Is it Glenn Miller or Tchaikovsky tonight?' The instruments huddled miserably in the arms of their players feeling very poorly indeed.

The conductor tapped the rostrum with his baton and announced, 'Beethoven!' The musicians raised their bows, elbows, drumsticks and reeds. The baton dropped.

But nothing happened.

The first violin croaked a hoarse note, and was silent. The gong shivered. The clarinets sighed. Then they too wheezed and lost their voices completely.

However hard the brass players blew, the string players bowed or the drummers banged, the orchestra only groaned and rattled unhappily to itself.

Soon the audience got cross and began to leave. The manager apologized and promised to give them their money back. The musicians cuddled their instruments and wept into them – big salt tears that made matters rather worse.

'I thought mine felt cold this evening,' sobbed the French horn player, polishing the chilly brass.

'I saw water spots on the snare-drums,' sniffed the drummer, 'but I took no notice!'

'It must have been the storm last night. They're all chilled to the chord!'

'They may never play again!' cried the conductor. 'Oh, my poor orchestra!'

That night, the instruments were left lying on the stage. 'What will become of us?' squeaked the piccolo.

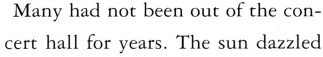

'Will we be replaced?' croaked the cello.

'Will others take our place under the stage?' snuffled the tuba.

The next day was bright and sunny. A bus arrived at the concert hall at twelve o'clock and all the sickly instruments, wrapped in blankets and rugs, were gently carried out-of-doors by the musicians.

Many had not been out of the concert hall for years. The sun dazzled on the silver section. The bassoon blinked its chrome keys. Outside the bus window, a symphony of colours flashed by.

'Are we going to be sold?' groaned the cello.

'Or scrapped?' wheezed the concert concertina tearfully.

'Or burned?' screamed the violins.

'Buried!' guessed the bassoon.

'Here will do,' said the conductor, who was driving the bus. 'Here will do nicely.'

He had stopped in the middle of the City Park between an ice cream van and a pile of deckchairs. Everyone got out.

The sun dappled through the trees. Birds sunbathed sleepily on the railings. People slept, with handkerchiefs over their faces. Everywhere was warm and sweet-smelling.

The musicians all sat down in deckchairs and let the sunlight dry out the drums, violins and the xylophone, the cello, clarinets and horn, the cymbals, tambourine and rusty triangle. The instruments steamed in the hot sun.

Then the conductor tapped his baton and whispered, 'Ladies? Gentlemen? Beethoven?' The musicians raised their bows, elbows, drumsticks and reeds . . .

Boom-boom-boom-BOOM!

A lazy flock of pigeons flew out of the trees. And a happy crowd gathered to listen to the first free concert ever given by the Royal Symphonic Orchestra in the City Park.

OSTRICHES CAN'T FLY

Jeremy Strong

NOT SO LONG ago, the ostriches had a king called Lionel. He was the biggest and best-looking ostrich in the whole of Africa. Wherever he went, the other ostriches cried, 'Oh! Just look at those legs! Aren't they the best legs in all Africa?'

And Lionel would look down at his great, knobbly knees and horny toes and agree with them. In fact, Lionel became very vain, and soon believed himself so clever he could do anything.

The other ostriches were too silly to see that Lionel was no better than any of them. Then one day, Lionel made a grand announcement.

'I can fly!'

There was uproar. No ostrich had ever been able to fly before! 'Oh! Show us! Oh, show us, O Great King!'

Lionel's heart plunged. Show them? He had not expected them to ask for a demonstration. What could he do?

'I can't show you today . . . er . . . the wind's blowing the wrong way.'

'Ah!' The birds nodded wisely. 'Never mind. We'll come back tomorrow to see you fly.'

Lionel thought it was a brilliant excuse, and the next morning, when the ostriches asked him to fly, he had his answer ready.

'I'm afraid the wind's still blowing the wrong way.'

'Oh!' they sighed with great disappointment. But the next day they arrived again. 'Oh, please fly for us today, O Great King!'

Lionel looked up at the sky and slowly shook his little head. 'The wind's *still* blowing the wrong way.'

A small voice spoke up. 'O King – if the wind's blowing the wrong way, why don't you turn round and fly in the other direction?'

Half the ostriches were so stunned by this amazing idea that they fainted. Others clapped their stumpy wings. But poor Lionel did not think it was a good idea at all. He would have to find a new excuse.

'There are too many clouds about!'

The ostriches shuffled about, sadly eyeing the sky. 'There's only one cloud.'

'One is quite enough.'

'It's a very *small* cloud,' one bird pointed out hopefully.

'It might look small from here, but when you get up close, it's enormous, believe me.'

'You needn't fly close to it,'

suggested another bird.

'Now look. I'm King. Don't tell me what to do. I can't fly when there's a cloud about.'

'O King!' wailed the ostriches, backing away. 'Please don't be angry. We only wish to see you fly. No ostrich has ever flown before!'

Lionel knew that sooner or later he would have to fly for them – otherwise they would realize he was lying and probably choose a new king. 'I'll definitely fly for you,' he announced at last, 'on Friday morning.'

'Hurray!'

Lionel had just three days to learn to fly. When nobody was looking, he ran up and down the sand flapping his tiny wings and jumping in the air. It was no use. His feathers flopped about like damp washing. He went and stood on a small hill, took a short run, and bravely leaped towards the sky.

'I can fly!' he cried. *Whumpp!*

He could not fly.

Bruised and battered all over, Lionel was feeling very sorry for himself, when all at once he had a brainwave. He hurried over to the lake and had a word with the flamingos.

'You could help – just tie a rope round my ankles, then fly off, towing me behind. It will all look quite real.'

The flamingos agreed to help, and Lionel was once more overcome by his cleverness. 'No wonder I'm King!'

On Friday morning, all the ostriches gathered to see their king fly. Lionel stood amongst the lakeside reeds to make his parting speech.

As he spoke, a pair of flamingos crept through the reeds and tied a rope round Lionel's ankles, as planned.

'Today,' cried Lionel, 'you will see a marvellous thing. I'll fly as no ostrich has flown in living memory. I'm so brave, so clever that . . . *Aaagh!*'

He never finished. The rope tightened and Lionel was

jerked off his feet. His chin bumped the sand, and he disappeared backwards into the reeds. At last he took to the air, dangling down from the rope. He swung gently to and fro, skimming the lake. Then the flamingos decided he was too heavy to carry – and dropped him.

The ostrich king plunged into the lake. He coughed, spluttered and struggled ashore, looking as if he had been in a washing-machine for a week. As soon as the other ostriches stopped laughing, they decided not to have a king any more. 'There's nothing special about Lionel,' they said. 'He's just as stupid as we are! Either we'll all be kings or all be ordinary ostriches.'

They decided to remain plain ostriches. Because they thought that if they were kings they might have to fly, and then they would look even sillier than they really were.

LITTLE RED RIDING-HOOD

Charles Perrault

ONCE UPON A TIME there lived a little country girl who was the prettiest ever seen. Her mother was immensely fond of her, and her grandmother, who loved her even more, made for her a little red riding-hood. This suited the little girl so well that everybody then called her Little Red Riding-Hood.

One day her mother, having made some custards, said to Little Red Riding-Hood, 'Go, my dear, and see how your grandmamma is feeling. She has been ill. Take her this custard and this little pot of butter.'

Little Red Riding-Hood set out at once to go to her grand-mother, who lived in another village.

As she was skipping through the wood, Little Red Riding-Hood met a wolf. The beast had a mind to eat her up at once, but he dared not because of some woodcutters near by in the forest. But he stopped her to ask her where she was going.

Little Red Riding-Hood, who did not know that it was dangerous to listen to a wolf, said to him, 'I am going to see my grandmamma and carry her a custard and a little pot of butter from my mamma.'

'Does she live far off?' asked the wolf.

'Oh, yes,' answered Little Red Riding-Hood. 'She lives

beyond that mill you see there, in the first house in the village.'

'Well,' said the wolf. 'I'll go and see her, too. I'll go this way and you go that. We shall see who will get there first.'

The wolf began to run as fast as he could, taking the nearest path. The little girl went by the longer route, and she stopped to gather nuts, run after butterflies, and pick flowers for a nosegay.

The wolf soon came to the old woman's house and knocked at the door – tap, tap.

'Who is there?' called an old woman's voice.

'It is your grandchild, Little Red Riding-Hood,' answered the wolf, disguising his voice. 'I've brought you a custard and a little pot of butter from Mamma.'

The good grandmother, who was still in bed because she was ill, cried out, 'Pull the bobbin, and the latch will go up.'

The wolf pulled the bobbin and the door opened. At once he fell upon the good woman and gobbled her down in a moment, for it had been more than three days since he had eaten. He then shut the door and lay in the grandmother's bed to await Little Red Riding-Hood.

Some time afterwards Little Red Riding-Hood knocked at the door – tap, tap.

'Who is there?'

Little Red Riding-Hood, hearing the big voice of the wolf, was at first afraid but she believed that her grandmother had a cold and thus was hoarse, so she answered, 'It is your grand-daughter, Little Red Riding-Hood. I have brought you a custard and a little pot of butter from Mamma.'

Softening his voice as much as he could, the wolf cried out now, 'Pull the bobbin, and the latch will go up.'

Little Red Riding-Hood pulled the bobbin, and the door opened.

The wolf, seeing her come in, said to her, as he hid under the bedclothes, 'Put the custard and the little pot of butter upon the stool, and come lie down with me.'

Little Red Riding-Hood came to the bed. But, seeing how strangely her grandmother looked, she said to her, 'Grandmamma, what great arms you have!'

'All the better to hug you with, my dear.'

'Grandmamma, what great ears you have!'

'All the better to hear you with, my dear.'

'Grandmamma, what great eyes you have!'

'All the better to see you with, my dear.'

'Grandmamma, what great teeth you have!'

'All the better to eat you with, my dear.'

And with these words, the wicked wolf fell upon Little Red Riding-Hood, and ate her up.

Now the wolf, having satisfied his hunger, went to sleep, snoring loudly. He snored so very loudly, indeed, that a hunter passing the house decided to enter to see if there was something wrong with the old woman.

When he walked up to her bed, he found the wolf. 'Aha,' he said, 'I have been looking for you a long time.' He saw that the wolf must have swallowed the grandmother and that she might yet be saved. He picked up a pair of shears and began to slit open the wolf's body. After a few snips, Little Red Riding-Hood appeared, and after a few more, out she jumped. Then out came the old grandmother.

All three were pleased. The huntsman took off the wolf's skin, and carried it home. The grandmother ate the custard, and Little Red Riding-Hood said she would never again pick flowers in the wood or listen to a wolf.

MISS DOSE THE DOCTORS' DAUGHTER

Allan Ahlberg

DORA DOSE WAS a doctor's daughter. Well, really she was a double doctor's daughter. Her mum was a doctor and her dad was a doctor. Dora liked to pretend *she* was a doctor.

Each morning, when her dad came down to breakfast, he said, 'Is there a doctor in the house?' And Dora shouted, 'Yes – me!' She took his temperature and tapped his knee with her little doctor's hammer. She told him to say 'Ah!'

Dora Dose had a pretend doctor's bag, a pretend doctor's waiting-room and six pretend patients. Dora's patients were: her little brother, her baby brother, her teddy, two dolls,

and – sometimes – the cat. Dora took their temperatures and tapped their knees with her little doctor's hammer. She told them to say 'Ah!'

But Dora was not happy being a pretend doctor. Her thermometer didn't really work. Her doctor's hammer was a toy. Her patients would not do as they were told.

'Next please!' said Dora. And her little brother said, 'It's *my* turn to be the doctor.'

'Next please!' said Dora. And her baby brother crawled off.

'Next please!' said Dora.

And the cat *ran* off.
'Next please!' said Dora. And the teddy and the dolls . . . just sat there.

'I wish I was a real doctor,' said Dora. And she went into the kitchen and bandaged up her mum.

Then — one morning — this happened. Dora Dose woke up and went into her baby brother's room. She was thinking of taking his temperature. But what did she find? Her baby brother was awake, smiling — and *covered in spots*!

'Oh!' said Dora. She ran into her little brother's room. He was covered in spots, too. Then she ran into her parents' room, and they were covered in spots.

'Is there a doctor in the house?' said Mr Dose.

And Dora said, 'Yes — me!'

'What we need is the spots medicine,' said Mrs Dose. She began to get out of bed.

'I'll go,' said Dora. Dora went downstairs to her mum and dad's surgery. She got the spots medicine. She gave her dad a spoonful, her mum a spoonful, her little brother a spoonful and her baby brother half a spoonful. She also tapped her baby brother's knee and told him to say 'Ah!' At nine o'clock Dora looked in her mum and dad's waiting-room. And what did she find? Lots of patients waiting – *real* patients – real *spotty* patients!

'What they need is the spots medicine,' said Mr Dose. He began to get out of bed.

'I'll go,' said Dora. Dora went downstairs to the surgery again. She put on her mum's white coat. She picked up her dad's stethoscope. She sat in the doctor's chair.

'Next please!' said Dora. And the first patient came in.

'You're a little doctor,' he said.

'Yes,' said Dora. She gave him a bottle of spots medicine.

'Next please!' said Dora. And the second patient came in.

'You're a *very* little doctor,' she said.

'Yes,' said Dora. She gave her *two* bottles.

'Next please!' said Dora. And the next patient came in –
and the next – and the next – and
the next. Most of them said
what a little doctor Dora was.
None of them said it was
their turn to be the doctor.
When all the patients had
gone, Dora Dose went
upstairs. She sat on her parents' bed. She took her dad's

temperature. She told her mum to say 'Ah!'

'Is there a doctor in the house?' said Dora.

'Yes,' said her dad.

And her mum said, 'You!'

A few days later, the doorbell rang at the doctors' house. Mr Dose opened the door. And what did he find? It was all those patients again. They had come to say 'thank you'. Their spots had gone.

'Is there a *little* doctor in the house?' they said.

'Well,' said Mr Dose, 'there's a little *spotty* doctor.'

And so there was. Doctor Dora was up in her room, as happy as could be. She had a real doctor's bag, a real thermometer, a real hammer . . .

. . . and a perfect patient – herself!

TICKY PICKY BOOM BOOM

Pat Thomson

ANANSE THE TRICKSTER had a very fine vegetable garden. He had every vegetable imaginable; plenty of potatoes and more yams than he could eat. But there was one thing he did not have: a flower garden, and Ananse wanted above all to have flowers, just like a rich man.

'I shall turn the yam patch into a flower garden,' he decided, 'and I shall make Mr Tiger dig the flower bed for me.'

Now Mr Tiger had been tricked by Ananse before and he was cautious.

'What will you give me if I dig out the yams?' he asked.

'You may keep all the yams you dig up,' replied Ananse.

Mr Tiger was satisfied with that. He loved to eat yams. So, early next morning, he began to dig Ananse's garden for him. All day, he dug and dug, but the harder he worked, the deeper the yams seemed to sink into the ground. By the end of the day, Ananse's garden was thoroughly turned over, but Mr Tiger had not been able to get any yams for himself at all.

Mr Tiger was hot, tired and furious. This was another of Ananse's tricks! He lost his temper and chopped at one of the yams. He chopped it into little pieces, and then set off for home, muttering angrily.

What was that?

Behind him, Mr Tiger heard a noise. A shuffling noise at first and then a stamping of small feet. Mr

Tiger turned around – and along the road behind him, walking on little vegetable legs, came the yams! The noise that their feet made went like this:

Ticky picky boom boom
Ticky picky boom boom
Ticky picky boom boom bouf!

Tiger began to run. The yams began to run, too.

Tiger began to gallop. The yams began to gallop.

Tiger jumped. The yams jumped.

Mr Tiger made straight for Mr Dog's house, running as fast as he could.

'Brother Dog,' he shouted, 'hide me! The yams are coming.'

'All right,' said Brother Dog. 'Hide behind me but don't say a word.'

So Mr Tiger hid behind Dog.

And down the road came the yams and the noise that their feet made sounded like this:

Ticky picky boom boom

Ticky picky boom boom

Ticky picky boom boom bouf!

The yams said, 'Brother Dog, have you seen Mr Tiger?'

And Brother Dog looked straight ahead and said, 'I can't see Mr Tiger anywhere, not at all.'

But Mr Tiger was so frightened that he called out, 'Don't

tell them, Brother Dog!' and Dog was so cross that he ran off and left Mr Tiger to the yams.

And the yams jumped. And Tiger jumped.

And the yams ran. And Tiger ran.

And the yams galloped. And Tiger galloped.

Then Mr Tiger saw Sister Duck and all her little ducklings, so he hurried up to her and said, 'Sister Duck, hide me! The yams are coming!'

'All right,' said Sister Duck. 'Get behind me but don't say a word.'

So Mr Tiger hid behind Sister Duck.

And down the road came the yams, and the noise that their feet made sounded like this:

Ticky picky boom boom
Ticky picky boom boom
Ticky picky boom boom bouf!

The yams said, 'Sister Duck, have you seen Mr Tiger?'

And Sister Duck looked straight ahead and said, 'Well now, I can't see him anywhere. Nowhere at all.'

But Mr Tiger was so frightened he shouted out, 'Don't tell

them, Sister Duck,' and Sister Duck was so cross that she moved away and left him to the yams.

And the yams jumped. And Tiger jumped.

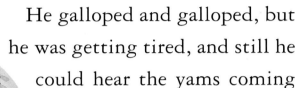

And the yams ran. And Tiger ran.

And the yams galloped. And Tiger galloped.

He galloped and galloped, but he was getting tired, and still he could hear the yams coming along the road behind him, getting nearer and nearer. At last, he came to a stream and over the stream was a little plank bridge. On the other side was Mr Goat.

Mr Tiger ran across the bridge and called out, 'Mr Goat, hide me! The yams are coming!'

'All right,' said Mr Goat, 'but don't say a word.'

So Mr Tiger hid behind Mr Goat.

And down the road came the yams, and the noise that their feet made sounded like this:

Ticky picky boom boom

Ticky picky boom boom

Ticky picky boom boom bouf!

When they reached the bridge, they called out, 'Mr Goat, have you seen Mr Tiger?'

And Mr Goat looked straight ahead but before he could say anything, Mr Tiger shouted, 'Don't tell them, Mr Goat, don't tell them.'

The yams jumped on to the bridge but so did Mr Goat, and he just put down his head and butted them into the stream. Then Mr Goat and Mr Tiger picked the pieces out of the water and took them home to make a great feast of yams. But they certainly did *not* invite Ananse to the feast.

When the nights are dark, Mr Tiger stays at home. He dare not walk along the road, for behind him, he still thinks he hears a noise which sounds like this:

Ticky picky boom boom
Ticky picky boom boom
Ticky picky boom boom bouf!

A Thousand Yards of Sea

Adèle Geras

THE FISHING BOAT was rocking slowly in the blue waters – to and fro, to and fro. Tom Taffet the fisherman looked at the heap of fish shining in the sun and thought, 'What a lot I've caught today! I shall haul in just one more catch and then make for the harbour.' He leaned over the edge of the little boat and drew in his net. As he poured the fish on to the deck, sparks of water slid from their pink-silvery, blue-silvery, brown speckled backs.

'There's a beauty,' thought Tom. 'I've never seen a fish that colour before.' He picked it up by the tail to have a closer

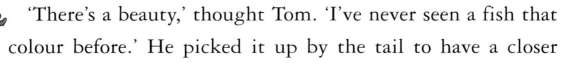

look, and was so surprised that he sat down at once, right in the middle of his catch. He was holding the tail of a mermaid! Her hair was brown and hung with seaweed, her tail was mauve and blue and silver and green, and her eyes were the colour of stormy water.

'Cod steaks and shrimp tails!' he said. 'I thought mermaids lived only in stories and sea shanties. Am I dreaming?'

'Certainly not,' said the mermaid. 'I don't know who you are, but I'd be very grateful if you'd just put me back into the water. I was on my way home, you know.'

'But I can't put you back,' said Tom. 'I could be rich if you would help me. We'd both be famous. I'd be able to buy a little house with a garden. I could grow flowers, and I'd never have to go fishing in the cold and the wind again.'

'That sounds lovely for you,' said the mermaid, 'but I

should hate it. I'd have to live in a glass box full of water and people would stare at me through the walls. I'd never see my family again.'

'I would look after you as if you were my own daughter,' said Tom. 'You could live with me and my wife. We'd put your tank in the front room and I'd bring you wonderful toys and good things to eat.'

'Would you like your daughter to live at the bottom of the sea?' asked the mermaid. 'However many good things she had down there, wouldn't you miss her?' She began to cry. Tears like small pearls rolled down her cheeks and plopped on to the fish piled up on the deck.

The fisherman thought for a long time. His daughter was grown up with children of her own, but he could still remember how she used to cry when she was small. He would have hated to have her live at the bottom of the sea. He would have missed her very much.

'Oh, well,' he sighed. 'I suppose you're right. You are too young to leave home. It's a shame, that's what it is. No one will believe that I've seen you. They'll say I was dreaming.'

'I'll give you something in return for setting me free,' said the mermaid, smiling now. 'And maybe they'll believe you, after all. May I borrow your knife?'

'It's very sharp. Please be careful,' said Tom. He picked up the mermaid and slipped her gently into the water. Then he put his knife in her hand. With a flash of her tail, she was gone.

'That's that then,' said Tom to himself. 'No mermaid and no knife. What a fool I am! Maybe I was dreaming, but my knife is gone and that's a pity. I shall have to buy a new one in the market tomorrow.' He turned the little boat towards the harbour. It was night-time now and Tom could see the reflection of the stars dancing in the black water.

Suddenly he heard a voice

say, 'Please don't go so quickly. I'm carrying something very heavy.' It was the mermaid. Tom was so surprised that he spilled a mug of cocoa all over his boots.

'Fish cakes and fillets!' he said. 'I never thought to see you again. What's that you're holding?'

'It's a thousand yards of sea. I've rolled it up and tied it neatly. I'm sure on land people would like to buy some. And here's your knife too.' She carried the bundle of sea into the boat, and handed the knife to Tom.

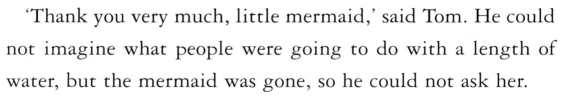

'Thank you very much, little mermaid,' said Tom. He could not imagine what people were going to do with a length of water, but the mermaid was gone, so he could not ask her.

The next day, Tom went to market to try to sell a few yards of sea. He set the bundle on a big wooden box and cut

the ropes of seaweed that the mermaid had tied so carefully. Wave upon wave of blue and green and silver fell around his feet. The colours shone and shifted and merged into one another.

'Come and buy! Come and buy! Genuine yards of sea, cut by a mermaid, yes a mermaid, just for me,' he shouted. 'Guaranteed to bring luck! Lovely colours! Come and see the lovely colours!'

People gathered round Tom's box and the women began to buy the silky, whispery stuff. At the end of the day, Tom Taffet had made enough money to buy a little house with a garden to grow flowers in.

The women made the yards of sea into dresses and petticoats that sounded like rushing water when they moved. And they called it taffeta, after Tom Taffet who brought it to the shore.

THE GINGERBREAD MAN

Traditional

ONCE UPON A TIME there was a little old woman and a little old man, and they lived all alone. They were very happy together, but they wanted a child and since they had none, they decided to make one out of gingerbread. So one day the little old woman and the little old man made themselves a little gingerbread man, and they put him in the oven to bake.

When the gingerbread man was done, the little old woman opened the oven door and pulled out the pan. Out jumped the little gingerbread man — and away he ran. The little old woman and the little old man ran after him as fast as they could, but he just laughed and said, 'Run, run, as fast as you can. You can't catch me! I'm the Gingerbread Man!'

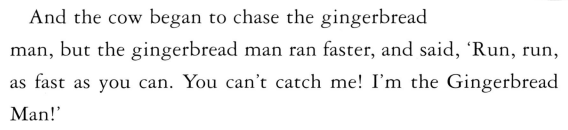

And they couldn't catch him.

The gingerbread man ran on and on until he came to a cow.

'Stop, little gingerbread man,' said the cow. 'I want to eat you.'

But the gingerbread man said, 'I have run away from a little old woman and a little old man, and I can run away from you, too. I can, I can!'

And the cow began to chase the gingerbread man, but the gingerbread man ran faster, and said, 'Run, run, as fast as you can. You can't catch me! I'm the Gingerbread Man!'

And the cow couldn't catch him.

The gingerbread man ran on until he came to a horse.

'Please, stop, little gingerbread man,' said the horse. 'I want to eat you.'

And the gingerbread man said, 'I have run away from a little old woman, a little old man, and a cow, and I can run away from you, too. I can, I can!'

And the horse began to chase the gingerbread man, but the gingerbread man ran faster and called to the horse, 'Run, run, as fast as you can. You can't catch me! I'm the Gingerbread Man!'

And the horse couldn't catch him.

By and by the gingerbread man came to a field full of farmers.

'Stop,' said the farmers. 'Don't run so fast. We want to eat you.'

But the gingerbread man said, 'I have run away from a little old woman, a little old man, a cow, and a horse, and I can run away from you, too. I can, I can!'

And the farmers began to chase him, but the gingerbread man ran faster than ever and said, 'Run, run, as fast as you can. You can't catch me! I'm the Gingerbread Man!'

And the farmers couldn't catch him.

The gingerbread man ran faster and faster. He ran past a school full of children.

'Stop, little gingerbread man,' said the children. 'We want to eat you.'

But the gingerbread man said, 'I have run away from a little old woman, a little old man, a cow, and a horse, a field full of farmers, and I can run away from you, too. I can, I can!'

And the children began to chase him, but the gingerbread man ran faster as he said, 'Run, run, as fast as you can. You can't catch me! I'm the Gingerbread Man!'

And the children couldn't catch him.

By this time the gingerbread man was so proud of himself he didn't think anyone could catch him. Pretty soon he saw a fox. The fox looked at him and began to run after him. But the gingerbread man said, 'You can't catch me! I have run away from a little old woman, a little old man, a cow, a horse, a field full of farmers, a school full of children, and I can run away from you, too. I can, I can! Run, run, as fast as you can. You can't catch me! I'm the Gingerbread Man!'

'Oh,' said the fox, 'I do not want to catch you. I only want to help you run away.'

Just then the gingerbread man came to a river. He could not swim across, and he had to keep running.

'Jump on my tail,' said the fox. 'I will take you across.'

So the gingerbread man jumped on the fox's tail, and the fox began to swim across the river. When he had gone a little way, he said to the gingerbread man, 'You are too heavy on my tail. Jump on my back.'

And the gingerbread man did.

The fox swam a little further, and then he said, 'I am afraid you will get wet on my back. Jump on my shoulder.'

And the gingerbread man did.

In the middle of the river, the fox said, 'Oh, dear, my shoulder is sinking. Jump on my nose, and I can hold you out of the water.'

So the little gingerbread man jumped on the fox's nose, and the fox threw back his head and snapped his sharp teeth.

'Oh, dear,' said the gingerbread man, 'I am a quarter gone!'

Next minute he said, 'Now I am half gone!'

And next minute he said, 'Oh, my goodness gracious! I am three quarters gone!'

And then the gingerbread man never said anything more at all.

BLESSU

Dick King-Smith

Blessu was a very small elephant when he sneezed for the first time.

The herd was moving slowly through the tall elephant-grass, so tall that it hid the legs of his mother and his aunties, and reached halfway up the bodies of his bigger brothers and sisters.

But you couldn't see Blessu at all.

Down below, where he was walking, the air was thick with pollen from the flowering elephant-grasses, and suddenly Blessu felt a strange tickly feeling at the base of his very small trunk.

Shutting his eyes and closing his mouth, he stuck his very small trunk straight out before him, and sneezed:

'AAARCHOOO!'

It wasn't the biggest sneeze in the world, but it was very big for a very small elephant.

'BLESS YOU!' cried his mother and his aunties and his bigger brothers and sisters.

For a moment Blessu looked rather cowed. He did not know what they meant, and he thought he might have done something naughty. He hung his head and his ears drooped.

But the herd moved on through the tall elephant-grass without taking any further notice of him, so he soon forgot to be unhappy.

Before long Blessu gave another sneeze, and another, and another, and each time he sneezed, his mother and his aunties and his bigger brothers and sisters cried:

'BLESS YOU!'

They did not say this to any of the other elephants, Blessu

noticed (because none of the other elephants sneezed), so he thought, 'That must be my name.'

At last the herd came out of the tall elephant-grass and went down to the river, to drink and to bathe, and Blessu stopped sneezing.

'Poor baby!' said his mother, touching the top of his hairy little head gently with the tip of her trunk. 'You've got awful hay fever.'

'And what a sneeze he's got!' said one of his aunties. 'It's not the biggest sneeze in the world, but it's very big for a very small elephant.'

The months passed, and Blessu grew, very slowly, as elephants do. But so did his hay fever. Worse and worse it got and more and more he sneezed as the herd moved through the tall elephant-grass.

Every few minutes Blessu would shut his eyes and close his mouth and stick his very small trunk straight out before him and sneeze:

'AAAARCHOOOO!!'

And each time he sneezed, his mother and his aunties and his bigger brothers and sisters cried:

'BLESS YOU!'

But though Blessu was not growing very fast, one bit of him was.

It was his trunk. All that sneezing was stretching it.

Soon he had to carry it tightly curled up, so as not to trip on it.

'Poor baby!' said his mother. 'At this rate your trunk will soon be as long as mine.'

But Blessu only answered:

'AAAARCHOOOO!!'

'Don't worry, my dear,' said one of his aunties. 'The longer the better, I should think. He'll be able to reach higher up into the trees than any elephant ever has, and he'll be able to go deeper into the river (using his trunk as a snorkel).'

'Ah well,' said Blessu's mother. 'Soon the elephant-grass will finish flowering, and the poor little chap will stop sneezing.'

And it did.

And he did.

The years passed, and each year brought the season of the

flowering of the elephant-grasses, that shed their pollen and made Blessu sneeze.

And each sneeze stretched that trunk of his just a little bit further.

By the time he was five years old, he could reach as high into the trees, and go as deep into the river (using his trunk as a snorkel) as his mother and his aunties.

By the time he was ten years old, he could reach higher and go deeper.

And by the time Blessu was twenty years old, and had grown a fine pair of tusks, he had, without doubt, the longest trunk of any elephant in the whole of Africa.

And now, in the season of the flowering of the elephant-grasses, what a sneeze he had!

Shutting his eyes and closing his mouth, he stuck his amazingly long trunk straight out before him and sneezed:

'AAAAAARCHOOOOOO!!!'

Woe betide anything that got in the way of that sneeze!

Young trees were uprooted, birds were blown whirling into the sky, small animals like antelope and gazelle were bowled over and over, larger creatures such as zebra and wildebeest stampeded in panic before that mighty blast, and even the King of Beasts took care to be out of the line of fire of the biggest sneeze in the world.

So if ever you should be in Africa when the elephant-grass is in flower, and should chance to see a great tusker with the longest trunk you could possibly imagine – keep well away, and watch, and listen.

You will see that great tusker shut his eyes and close his mouth and stick his fantastically, unbelievably, impossibly long trunk straight out before him. And you will hear:

'AAAAAARCHOOOOOO!!!'

And then you know what to say, don't you?

'BLESSU!'

HEDGEHOGS DON'T EAT HAMBURGERS

Vivian French

Hector saw a picture on a paper bag.

'What's that?' he asked.

'That's a hamburger,' said his dad.

'Can I have one for my tea?' asked Hector.

'No,' said his dad. 'Hedgehogs don't eat hamburgers.'

'I do,' said Hector. 'And I'm going to go and find one for my tea.'

Hector set off to find a hamburger.

'Here I go, here I go, here I go,' he sang as he walked along.

Hattie popped out to see who was going by.

'Hello,' said Hector. 'I'm going to find my tea.'

'Would you like some fine fat snails?' Hattie asked.

'No thank you,' said Hector. 'I'm going to find a hamburger.'

'Hedgehogs don't eat hamburgers,' said Hattie.

'I do,' said Hector.

'Oh,' said Hattie. 'Maybe I'll come too.'

So she did.

Hector and Hattie set off to find a hamburger.

'Here we go, here we go, here we go,' they sang as they walked along.

Harry popped out to see who was going by.

'Hello,' said Hector. 'We're going to find my tea.'

'Would you like some slow slimy slugs?' Harry asked. 'I've got plenty.'

'No thank you,' said Hector. 'I'm going to find a hamburger.'

'Hedgehogs don't eat hamburgers,' said Harry.

'I do,' said Hector.

'Oh,' said Harry. 'Maybe I'll come too.'

So he did.

Hector and Hattie and Harry set off to find a hamburger.

'Here we go, here we go, here we go,' they sang as they walked along.

Hester popped out to see who was going by.

'Hello,' said Hector. 'We're going to find my tea.'

'Would you like some big black beetles?' Hester asked. 'I've got lots.'

'No thank you,' said Hector. 'I'm going to find a hamburger.'

'Hedgehogs don't eat hamburgers,' said Hester.

'I do,' said Hector.

'Oh,' said Hester. 'Maybe I'll come too.'

So she did.

Hector and Hattie and Harry and Hester set off to find a hamburger.

'Here we go, here we go, here we go,' they sang as they walked along.

Fox popped out to see who was going by.

'Hello,' said Hector. 'We're going to find my tea.'

'Tea, eh?' said Fox. 'What a good idea.' He looked at the fat little hedgehogs, and he licked his lips.

'I'm going to find a hamburger,' said Hector.

'WHAT a good idea,' said Fox. 'Shall I show you the way?'

'YES PLEASE,' said Hector.

Hector and Hattie and Harry and Hester set off after Fox.

'Here we go, here we go, here we go,' they sang as they walked along.

'SSSHHH!' said Fox.

'Oh,' said Hector and Hattie and Harry and Hester.

They walked up the hill and down the hill.

'Are we nearly there?' asked Hector.

'Nearly,' said Fox. He sniffed the air. 'Yes, we're nearly there.'

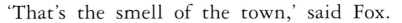

Hector sniffed the air too.

'What is it?' he asked.

'That's the smell of the town,' said Fox. 'That's where the hamburgers are.'

'Oh,' said Hector. He sniffed the air again. He could smell cars, and smoke, and shops, and houses. He could smell danger. 'Maybe I don't want a hamburger today. Maybe I'll have big black beetles or slow slimy slugs, or fine fat snails. Maybe hedgehogs don't eat hamburgers after all.'

Hector turned round, and Hattie and Harry and Hester all turned round too.

'Here we go, here we go, here we go!' they sang.

'JUST A MINUTE,' said Fox, and he opened his mouth wide. His teeth were sharp and white. 'What about MY tea?'

'YOU can have a hamburger,' said Hector.

'But I don't WANT a hamburger,' said Fox. 'I want little fat HEDGEHOGS!' And he jumped at Hector and Hattie and Harry and Hester.

'HERE WE GO, HERE WE GO, HERE WE GO,' sang all four little hedgehogs, and they rolled themselves up tightly into four prickly balls.

'OWWWW!' said Fox as he hurt his nose. 'OW! OW! OW!' He turned round and ran up the hill and down the hill. He didn't stop running until he got home to his mummy.

Hector and Hattie and Harry and Hester looked at each other.

'Let's go home,' said Hector.

So they all set off to go home.

'Home we go, home we go, home we go,' they sang as they walked up the hill and down the hill. And they got home just in time to have fine fat snails, slow slimy slugs and big black beetles for their tea.

MRS SIMKIN'S BATHTUB

Linda Allen

'ARE YOU AWARE,' said Mr Simkin to Mrs Simkin one morning, 'that the bathtub's halfway down the stairs?'

'How very inconvenient,' said Mrs Simkin, going to have a look. 'How long has it been there?'

'I have no idea,' said Mr Simkin. 'It was in the bathroom when I went to bed last night, and now it's here, so it must have moved when we were asleep.'

'Well, we shall just have to make the best of it,' said Mrs Simkin. 'Will you bathe first, or shall I?'

'I will,' said Mr Simkin bravely.

He stepped into the bathtub. It wobbled a bit at first, but it soon settled down. Mrs Simkin fetched soap and towels, shampoo and bath salts, and arranged them nicely on the stairs. 'There,' she said, 'it doesn't look too bad now, and if I polish the taps and scrub the feet, it should look quite smart. I'm sure none of the neighbours has a bathtub on the stairs.'

Mr Simkin said she was probably right.

After a day or two they hardly noticed that the bathtub was there at all. It didn't really inconvenience them to squeeze past it when they went upstairs, and the landing smelled so pleasantly of bath salts that Mrs Simkin began to feel quite happy about it.

She invited the lady next door to have a look, but the lady next door said that she didn't approve of these modern ideas.

One morning, Mr Simkin went to have his bath. 'My dear!' he cried. 'Come and see! The bathtub's gone!'

'Gone!' cried Mrs Simkin, leaping out of bed. 'Gone where?'

'I don't know,' said Mr Simkin, 'but it isn't on the stairs.'

'Perhaps it's back in the bathroom,' said Mrs Simkin.

They went to look, but it wasn't there.

'We shall have to buy another one,' said Mr Simkin as they went down to breakfast.

The bathtub was in the kitchen.

'You know, my dear,' said Mr Simkin a few minutes later, 'this is a much better place for a bathtub than halfway down the stairs. I quite like having breakfast in the bath.'

'Yes,' agreed Mrs Simkin, 'I quite like it here too. The bath towels match the saucepans.'

'That's a very good point,' said Mr Simkin.

One day Mr and Mrs Simkin went downstairs to find that the bathtub had moved again. It was in the living room, sitting smugly before the fire.

'Oh, I don't think I like

it there,' said Mrs Simkin, 'but I don't suppose it will stay there very long. Once a bathtub has started to roam, it never knows when to stop.'

She was quite right. The next day they found it in the cellar, with spiders in it.

One day they couldn't find the bathtub anywhere.

'What shall I do?' cried Mrs Simkin. 'It's my birthday, and I did so want to use that lovely bubble bath you gave me.'

'So did I,' said Mr Simkin.

The lady next door came round. 'Happy birthday,' she said. 'Did you know that your bathtub was on the front lawn?'

They all went to have a look.

There was a horse drinking out of it.

'Go away,' said Mrs Simkin. 'How dare you drink my bath water, you greedy creature.'

She stepped into the bathtub. The lady next door said she didn't know what the world was coming to, and she went

home and locked herself indoors.

As the bubbles floated down the street, lots of people came to see what was going on. They were very interested.

They leaned on the fence and watched.

They asked if they could come again.

One day when there was rather a chilly wind about, they found the bathtub in the greenhouse. Everyone was very disappointed.

'My dear,' said Mr Simkin a few days later, 'do you happen to know where the bathtub is today?'

'No,' said Mrs Simkin, 'but today's Tuesday. It's quite often in the garage on Tuesdays.'

'It isn't there today,' said Mr Simkin. 'I've looked everywhere.'

'I do hope it hasn't gone next door,' sighed Mrs Simkin. 'The lady next door has no sympathy at all.'

Mr Simkin went round to inquire.

The lady next door said she was of the opinion that people ought to be able to control their bathtubs.

Mr Simkin went home.

Mr Robinson from across the street rang up. 'I know it's none of my business,' he said, 'but I thought you'd like to know that your bathtub is on the roof of your house.'

Mr Simkin went up to take his bath. All the people cheered.

The bathtub seemed to like being up there, because that's where it stayed.

The people in the street had a meeting in Mr Simkin's greenhouse. They decided to have their bathtubs on the roofs of their houses too.

All except the lady next door.

She preferred to take a shower.

THE HORRENDOUS HULLABALOO

Margaret Mahy

THERE WAS ONCE a cheerful old woman who kept house for her nephew, Peregrine – a pirate by profession.

Every morning she put on her pirate pinafore, poured out Peregrine's ration of rum, picked up his socks, and petted his parrot. She worked day in, day out, keeping everything ship-shape.

Meanwhile, her pirate nephew went out to parties every night, though he never once asked his aunt or his parrot if they would like to go with him.

Whenever his aunt suggested that she and the parrot might

want to come too, Peregrine replied, 'You wouldn't enjoy pirate parties, dear aunt. The hullabaloo is horrendous!'

'But I like horrendous hullabaloos!' exclaimed the aunt. 'And so does the parrot.'

'When I come back from sea I want a break from the parrot,' said Peregrine, looking proud and piratical. 'And if I took my aunt to a party, all the other pirates would laugh at me.'

'Very well,' thought his aunt, 'I shall have a party of my own.'

Without further ado she sent out masses of invitations written in gold ink. Then she baked batch after batch of delicious rumblebumpkins while the parrot hung upside down on a pot plant, clacking its beak greedily.

No sooner had Peregrine set off that evening on another night's hullabaloo than his aunt, shutting the door behind him, peeled off her pirate pinafore and put on her patchwork party dress.

'Half-past seven!' she called to the parrot. 'We'll soon be having a horrendous hullabaloo of our own!'

Then she opened the windows and sat waiting for the guests to come, enjoying the salty scent of the sea, and the sound of waves washing around Peregrine's pirate ship, out in the moonlit bay.

'Half-past eight!' chimed the clock. The pirate's aunt waited.

'Half-past nine!' chimed the clock. The pirate's aunt still waited, shuffling her feet and tapping her fingers.

'Half-past ten!' chimed the clock. The rumblebumpkins were in danger of burning. No one, it seemed, was brave enough to come to a party at a pirate's house. The pirate's aunt shed bitter tears over the rumblebumpkins.

Suddenly the parrot spoke. 'I have lots of friends who love rumblebumpkins,' she cackled. 'Friends who aren't put in a panic or petrified by pirates – friends who would happily help with a hullabaloo!'

'Well, what are you waiting for?' cried the pirate's aunt. 'Go and fetch them at once!'

Out of the window the parrot flew, while the aunt mopped up her tears and patted powder on her nose.

Almost at once the night air was filled with flapping and fluttering. The sea swished and sighed. The night breeze smelled of passion-fruit, pineapples and palm trees. In through the open windows tumbled the patchwork party

guests, all screeching with laughter. They were speckled, they were freckled; they were streaked and striped like the rollicking rags of rainbow. All the parrots in town had come to the aunt's party.

'Come one, come all!' the aunt cried happily.

The parrots cackled loudly, breaking into a bit of a sing-song. So loud was the sing-song that the pirate's neighbours all rushed out of their houses, prepared for the worst.

'What a horrendous hullabaloo!' they cried in amazement.

The aunt invited them all to feast richly on her rumble-bumpkins, and to join her in a wild jig. She was having a wonderful time.

When Peregrine arrived home later that night, his house was still ringing with leftover echoes of a horrendous hulla-baloo. The air smelled strongly of rumblebumpkins, and the floor was covered with parrot feathers.

'Aunt!' he called crossly. 'Come

and tidy up at once.'

But there was no one at home for, at that very moment, his aunt, still wearing her patchwork party dress, was stealing away on Peregrine's own pirate ship.

Over the moonlit sea she was sailing, with parrots perched all over her, making a horrendous hullabaloo. As they sailed off in search of passion-fruit, pineapples and palm trees, it was impossible to tell where the aunt left off and the parrots began.

So left on his own, with a grunt and a groan, Peregrine put on the pirate pinafore and tidied up for himself.

HOW THE LEOPARD GOT HIS SPOTS

Traditional

ALONG TIME AGO, the leopard had no spots, the zebra had no stripes, and the hyena was the most beautiful and proud animal in the jungle. But now these animals look very different, and this is how it happened.

One day Hyena was running through the jungle when he saw Tortoise gazing up at the fruit hanging from a tree above his head.

'Hyena,' cried Tortoise, 'please will you come and shake this tree with your strong paws, and bring down some of the fruit. I am so hungry, but the branches are too high for me to reach.'

Hyena laughed, baring his sharp white teeth.

'Of course I'll help you, Tortoise,' he said. 'I'll put you right up into the branches of the tree so that you can reach the fruit yourself.' Taking Tortoise between his strong jaws, he picked him up and put him on a branch high above the ground. Then off he ran, laughing at the poor, helpless tortoise.

Tortoise sat in the tree all day, afraid to move in case he fell. He was afraid to stretch out for any of the fruit. Hungry and tired, he was still there by the time the sun had nearly set.

Then, swiftly and silently, Leopard bounded out of the twilight.

'Leopard! Leopard!' called Tortoise. 'Help! I'm stuck! I can't get down from this tree by myself.'

Leopard smiled kindly and immediately leaped up into the

tree. He gently lifted Tortoise in his mouth and then jumped down again.

'Can I do anything else for you, Tortoise?' he asked.

'I'm very hungry,' said Tortoise. 'Could you shake the tree so that some of the fruit falls down?'

'Of course,' said Leopard, and he shook the tree until all the fruit had fallen to the ground.

Tortoise would have plenty to eat for days and days.

Leopard was just about to run off into the darkness when Tortoise stopped him. 'I'd like to give you a present, Leopard,' he said, 'just to thank you. If you come back tomorrow when it's light, I will make you the most beautiful, the most magnificent animal in the whole jungle.'

The next morning Leopard returned and found Tortoise waiting for him with a box of paints and some paintbrushes.

'Leopard,' he said, 'I'm going to give you the most beautiful coat in the world. You will be the envy of every animal in the jungle.' And with his paints, Tortoise painted Leopard's coat with a rich and exotic pattern of dark spots.

When Tortoise had finished, Leopard walked away through the jungle. All the animals turned their heads and admired his beautiful new coat, and when Zebra saw him, he decided that he would go to Tortoise, too, and ask for a new coat.

'Please, Tortoise,' he said, 'will you paint my coat so that I look as beautiful as Leopard?'

Tortoise looked at him thoughtfully for a moment. Then

he picked up his paints and painted Zebra's coat with stripes of black and white. When Tortoise had finished, Zebra galloped happily back into the jungle and all the animals congratulated him on his lovely new coat.

Now Hyena was very jealous when he saw how beautiful Leopard and Zebra looked, and he decided that he would go to Tortoise and pretend to be sorry for leaving him in the fruit tree. Then perhaps Tortoise would give him a lovely coat as well.

So off Hyena went to Tortoise, and said how sorry he was, and asked if Tortoise would paint his coat like Zebra and Leopard's.

Tortoise smiled.

'Certainly,' he said and picked up his paints. He painted for many hours, standing back from time to time to admire his

work. When he had finished he sent Hyena off to show his new coat to all the other animals.

Hyena pranced proudly back into the jungle, his head held high. But all the animals just laughed and jeered at him. And when Hyena caught sight of his new coat in the river he knew why. Tortoise had painted his coat with a mess of dirty brown blotches. He was now the ugliest animal in the jungle.

Hyena slunk away into the furthest, darkest corner of the jungle to hide himself in shame. And to this very day hyenas only come out at night when no one can see their coats.

PUFFLING IN A PICKLE

Margaret Ryan

I T WAS PUFFLING'S first day out of the burrow, and he was
ready to explore.

'Don't wander off and get lost,' said his mum.

'I won't,' said Puffling.

'Remember to stay close to home,' said his dad.

'I will,' said Puffling.

And he really meant to.

But he forgot.

There were so many interesting things to see elsewhere.

First, there was a very interesting cliff top to peer over.

'What a long way down to the beach,' said Puffling, waving to the seals below.

Then there was a very interesting empty crisp packet to investigate; till it blew away in the wind.

'Come back,' squawked Puffling, and chased after it.

Finally, there was a big grassy hill to climb.

'I wonder what's on the other side,' said Puffling, and puffed up the hill to see.

All he saw was the other side of the grassy hill.

'Well, that's not very interesting,' said Puffling. 'I think I'll go home now.'

He waddled back down the hill and looked at all the burrows.

'Now which one is mine?' he wondered. 'There are so many . . . I think it might be this one.'

He poked his fluffy head down to see.

'Mum,' he called, 'are you in there?'

'I'm not your mum, you silly bird,' squawked a very cross puffin. 'Go and find your own burrow, and stop poking your beak down other people's. What a cheek. Really, young birds these days . . . no manners at all.'

'Sorry,' said Puffling, and scuttled away.

He wandered on till he found another burrow that looked familiar.

'Maybe this is mine,' he said.

He poked his fluffy head down to see.

'Mum, Dad, are you in there?' he called.

'What a silly billy bird,' scoffed a family of rabbits. 'Are you blind? Do we look like your mum and dad? Do we have wings? Do we have feathers? Do we have orange beaks?'

'No, but you do rabbit on a bit,' muttered Puffling and scuttled away.

Puffling wandered on till he came to quite a large burrow near the cliff.

'I don't know if this is my burrow or not,' he panted, 'but I think I'll just slip inside for a rest anyway. I'm tired out with all this exploring.'

He went down into the burrow and called, 'Mum? Dad? Is there anybody in there?'

'Who wants to know?' answered an oily voice.

'Me, Puffling. I'm tired out. I'm looking for my burrow, and I can't find it anywhere. I think it's lost.'

'Oh, what a shame,' said the oily voice. 'Come on in, and rest yourself, little Puffling. You'll be very comfortable in here, and you're VERY welcome.'

'Thank you,' said Puffling, and went on in.

Then he saw whose burrow it was.

'Sly fox!' he yelled, and turned and ran outside.

Sly fox bounded after him.

'Come back, little Puffling,' he called. 'You'll be just right for my dinner.'

'Oh no, he won't,' squawked a familiar voice, and Puffling's dad dropped down from the sky, and nipped sly fox on the nose.

'OOOOOOWWWWLLLL!'

'This way, Puffling,' squawked his mum. 'FLY!'

And Puffling flew, his little wings flapping as fast as they would go.

'Whew, that was a lucky escape,' said his dad when they were all safely back inside their own burrow.

'I thought I told you not to wander off and get lost, Puffling,' said his mum. 'Your dad and I have been out looking for you for ages.'

'I'm sorry,' said Puffling. 'I tried to get home, but then all the burrows looked the same.'

'I have an idea,' said his dad. 'Come outside . . . See that big tree over there . . .?'

Puffling nodded.

'Well, our burrow is the third one on the left after the big tree. Right?'

'No, left,' grinned Puffling.

Cold Feet

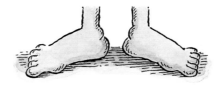

Susan Eames

ONCE UPON A TIME, there were a King and Queen. Most of the time, they were very happy. The only trouble was that the King was terribly untidy – he would keep leaving his clothes all over the palace.

'If you leave ANY more clothes lying around,' said the Queen one morning, as she picked up a jumper, some hats and a coat off the bedroom floor, 'or lose your socks again – I'll – I'll – I won't make any more special fruit cake for tea!' And she stormed out.

'Oh dear,' said the King to himself, 'I'd better not tell her I've lost my crown and my socks. I couldn't go without my fruit cake. I wonder where the crown can be?'

And he sat down on his throne, to have a think.

'Ow!' The King leaped up again – and looked at his throne. There was his crown.

'Well, at least I've found *that*!' He put the crown on his head, and sat back on the throne. 'Now where have I left my socks?'

He thought and thought. It was no good. He couldn't even think where he'd left one sock.

He hunted all round the royal bedroom – under the bed, inside the chest, on top of the wardrobe, even all through his dirty clothes. Not one sock to be found.

'Dear oh dear!' said the King. 'I dare not tell the Queen I've lost them. I shall have to think of a reason for not wearing them, that's all.'

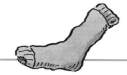

Then he had an idea. 'I know! I'll issue a proclamation – that's what kings do when they're in a spot of trouble.'

Next day, all over the palace there were large notices, proclaiming: 'NO SOCKS TO BE WORN IN THIS PALACE FOR A WEEK. SIGNED – THE KING.'

People were rather surprised, but if the King told them to take off their socks, then take them off they must. So, for a week, everyone in the palace, and everyone who came to the palace, went barefoot.

At the end of the week, the King, very pleased with his idea, was getting ready to write out a new proclamation to carry on for another week, when the Queen came in looking tearful over a large bundle of assorted socks.

'Something the matter, dear?' asked the King, as he signed his name with a flourish.

'It's all these socks,' said the Queen, shaking her head. 'Everybody who's come to visit the palace this week – the

milkman, the postman, the
baker, the King of Belgravia
and his son – they've all had
to take their socks off, and
leave them in a pile on the
doorstep. But the socks
always get mixed up, and
they all look alike –
nobody can find their own!
So they keep going home
barefoot.'

'Never mind, my dear,' said the King,
'at least the sock-maker in town will have a lot of work making new socks for everyone . . . Now I'll just go and get this
new proclamation printed . . .'

But at that moment, there was a knock at the palace door.

'I'll get it,' said the Queen. 'I expect it's the postman.'

She came back in a few moments with a letter and a large
parcel. 'They're for you,' she said, handing them to the King.

'I'll leave the parcel till last,' he said, opening the letter.
'Well, well, well! What a surprise! It's from Fred Needle –
Maker of Best Quality Socks!'

'Is he pleased with the work he's been getting?' asked the Queen.

'Well, he says: "Your Majesty, I have been making socks night and day for the last week and I am VERY TIRED. Please will you cancel your proclamation, and let everyone keep their socks on again, because I need a rest." Signed, "Fred Needle, Sock Maker."'

'Poor man,' said the Queen. 'You will cancel the proclamation, won't you?'

'No, no!' said the King hurriedly. 'I couldn't possibly.' And he quickly opened the parcel. He couldn't believe his eyes. It was a box full of socks – different colours, different patterns, some short and some long.

'By jove!' said the King. 'These are rather nice – much nicer than any of the ones I lost – I mean, than any of the ones I'm not wearing at the moment.'

'They're from Fred Needle,' said the Queen, reading the note which was inside. 'He hopes you'll like them so much, you'll want to keep them on your feet and cancel the proclamation.'

'Splendid!' said the King, beaming from ear to ear. 'I'll wear this pair today, and that pair tomorrow . . .'

'But what about the proclamation?'

'Oh, cancel the proclamation!' said the King.

'Hurray!' said the Queen. 'I'll make some fruit cake for tea to celebrate.' And she rushed off to the kitchen.

The King tried on a pair of his new socks. 'Wonderful!' he exclaimed, wiggling his toes. 'It's going to take me a very long time to lose all these!' And he tore up his proclamation and went off to the kitchen to wait for the fruit cake.

THE FISH CART

Ruth Manning-Sanders

Fox crept under some bushes by the roadside. He was hungry. He hadn't eaten anything since yesterday at dinner time, and now it was dinner time again. *Sniff, sniff, sniff* went Fox's nose, poking among the bushes.

'We're wasting our time here,' said Fox's nose. 'There's been a rabbit, but he's gone.'

So Fox crept out from under the bushes on to the edge of the road. '*Sniff, sniff, sniff!* Oh, oh, now I *do* smell something!' whispered Fox's nose. 'I smell something delicious! I smell *fish*!'

And see, coming along the highroad towards Fox, a man driving a cart piled high with fish!

'My dinner, my dinner!' thought Fox, backing under the bushes again. 'But how to get it?'

Yes, indeed, how to get it?

The cart trundled slowly past. It was drawn by an old grey horse and driven by a man with a red face, who sat on one of the shafts roaring out a song.

'It's a low cart, we could easily spring up into it,' Fox's legs told him.

'And eat and eat and *eat*,' said Fox . . . 'But no, the man may have a gun, and then I should be dead before I'd swallowed a mouthful! . . . Dead, eh? Well now, that *is* an idea!'

So, as Fox sat thinking, who should come bounding over the hedge but Wolf. Wolf was hungry too; he was making an angry face and gnashing his teeth. 'Cousin Fox, Cousin Fox,' he snarled, 'find me something to eat this *minute* – or I shall eat *you*!'

Fox knew he was much cleverer than Wolf, so he wasn't frightened. 'Just keep calm, Cousin Wolf,' said he. 'Wait here, and I'll get you food – plenty of it.'

The fish cart had disappeared round a bend of the road, but it was going slowly. It wasn't very far ahead, so Fox's ears told him. They could still hear the rumble of the cartwheels, and the driver's loud song.

'Off with us then!' said Fox's legs, and they pushed through the hedge into a field, galloped faster than fast across the field, and came out again on to the highroad ahead of the fish cart. Then Fox lay down with his eyes shut, and his body stiff, and his legs sprawled out. He was pretending to be dead.

Along came the cart. The big man with the red face pulled up the old grey horse. What was that lying there? A dead fox, eh! And he jumped down from the shaft he was sitting on, picked up Fox, and tossed him into the cart on top of the fish. Then he scrambled on to the shaft again, and drove on.

'*Troll-a-loll, troll-a-loll!*' The man was roaring out a song about how he would skin Fox, and how his wife would make him a warm winter waistcoat of fox fur. His roaring voice, the rumble of the wheels, and the *clop, clop* of the horse's hoofs clattered about Fox's ears as he lay stretched out stiffly on top of the pile of fish pretending to be dead . . .

But what was Fox doing now? He was quietly, quietly moving his tail and flicking one fish after another out of the cart and down on to the road.

But what was Wolf doing? Well, Wolf had got tired of waiting. He had a smell of fish in his nostrils, and the smell was coming from somewhere along the highroad in front of him.

So away trotted Wolf, and he had just got round the bend of the road when – did you ever? – fish, *fish*, FISH, a strew of fish scattered ahead of him!

'Oh, my dinner, my dinner, my good dinner!' Wolf opened his mouth as wide as it would go, and began gulping down one fish after another. And on he went, and on he went gulping and gobbling . . .

The man sitting on the shaft of the cart was still singing about his Sunday waistcoat of fox fur. He didn't look behind him, no, not once. Fox pushed the last fish out of the cart, opened his eyes, gave a leap down on to the road and saw Wolf looking fat and pleased with himself, swallowing down the very last fish.

'Oh, Cousin Wolf, Cousin Wolf, you big greedy thief! There was enough fish for us both, more than enough for us both, and you've eaten them all!'

'Of course I've eaten them all,' said Wolf. 'You promised to get me plenty of food. You didn't say you wanted any yourself. And I'm really grateful to you, Cousin Fox,' said he, licking his lips and smiling fatly.

Fox was so angry that he flew at Wolf, thinking to bite him. But Wolf lifted his lip and snarled, so Fox thought better of it. Wolf was three times as big as he was.

'There are other ways!' he muttered.

Then he turned and trotted off home, with his poor empty stomach making grumbling noises, and his busy brain making plans to get his own back on greedy Wolf.

WIL'S TAIL

Hazel Hutchins

WILMOT JAMES EDWARD HUTCHINS was the sixth wolf from the left at the school Christmas Concert. When the concert was over everyone said what a good Christmas forest creature he'd been and everyone admired his costume. Wil admired his costume too – especially the tail.

It was a wonderful tail. His mother had made it from the belt of her old fake-fur coat. Wil himself had sewn it to the seat of his favourite corduroy trousers. It was the kind of tail that hung 'just right' and swung 'just right'. It was the kind of tail with which Wil could slink or jump; the kind of tail he

could twirl or drape; the kind of tail he could curl smoothly around him. It had patterns and lines and colours in it that Wil had never even thought about before, and it was softer than anything he'd ever known.

When Wil got home, he hung the wolf mask on his bedroom wall. He put the sweater (his dad's) back in the big dresser drawer. He put the mittens (his sister's) and the moccasins (his mother's) back in the closet where they belonged. But he kept the tail.

The next day was Christmas Eve. Wil helped wrap presents and eat biscuits. When evening came, his family went to a party at the neighbours'. Wil's dad wore his smart jeans. Wil's mum wore her party blouse. Wil's sister wore sixteen hair-slides. And Wil wore his tail.

He wore it during supper and he wore it during games and he wore it during carol singing. The neighbours thought it a bit strange, but they were too polite to say anything.

Wil was tired when he got home. He hung up his stocking

and rolled into bed. His tail rolled into bed too, all except the tip which hung out over the edge.

On Christmas morning, Wil's family hugged and kissed and opened presents and ate breakfast. They went to the cousins for the day. Wil's dad wore his Christmas tie. Wil's mum wore her Christmas perfume. Wil's sister wore her Christmas brooch and her Christmas socks. Wil wore his Christmas tail.

Aunt Beth nearly had a heart attack when she stepped on it in the kitchen.

On Boxing Day, the family ate leftovers and played 327 games of draughts. The next day they went shopping in the city. Everyone wore their everyday, ordinary clothes. Wil wore his tail.

The tip of it got caught in the escalator of Krumings' department store. A loud warning bell went off. Two security people and three maintenance personnel worked to free the mechanism and every shopper in the whole store came to see the boy whose tail had been caught between the second and third floors.

For the rest of the week Wil stayed at home with his tail. He repaired it with an extra piece, so it was longer than ever. He built a den in the basement. He took long naps in front of the fire with the cat. And he waited for New Year's Eve.

On New Year's Eve the family always went skating on Whitefish Lake. Wil was planning on wearing his tail. He could just see himself streaking down the lake in the darkness; the wind rushing smoothly against his face and his tail flying far out behind.

But when New Year's Eve came and he tried to tuck his tail up under his sweater, his mother looked at him and shook her head.

'No,' she said. 'It's dangerous. You'll trip over it and fall and so will everybody else.'

Wil appealed to his father.

'No,' he said. 'It's dangerous. When you go and warm up at the bonfire you're likely to set yourself ablaze.'

'But it's part of me!' said Wil.

His parents did not agree.

'All right,' said Wil. 'I'll wear it but I won't go skating and I won't go near the fire.'

His parents gave in.

Whitefish Lake on New Year's Eve was wonderful. People from all over came to skate and laugh and warm themselves around an enormous bonfire. Wil climbed a little hill between the lake and the river which flowed beyond. He listened to the wonderful sound of skate-blades on ice. He watched skaters passing hockey pucks, turning figures of eight, and playing tag. Just when he could stand it no longer and had decided to take off his tail and put on his skates, he heard shouting behind him.

'Someone's fallen through the river

ice!' called the man.

'We can't reach them. A rope. A long scarf. Help! Anyone, please!' called the woman.

Wil thought for only a moment. He reached behind him and pulled with all his might. With a rip his tail came loose. He raced down the slope. The woman took it without a word and disappeared into the darkness.

Wil never did get to go skating on Whitefish Lake that New Year's Eve. By the time all the excitement died down, it was time for his family to go home.

But he did get his tail back. The woman who'd taken it made a special point of bringing it back to him. It was sodden and torn and about four feet longer than it had been to start with. Wil didn't care. His tail had actually saved someone's life!

The tail sits, these days, curled up in a special place, right in the middle of Wil's bedroom shelf – an heroic Christmas tail.

THE THREE
BILLY GOATS GRUFF

Traditional

THREE GOATS ONCE lived together in a field. The littlest one was called Little Billy Goat Gruff. The next one was bigger than Little Billy Goat Gruff, so he was called Big Billy Goat Gruff. But the third was the biggest of them all, and he was called Great Big Billy Goat Gruff.

At the end of their field was a river, and across the river was another field. Now this field was empty and the grass there grew rich and long and very green. Little Billy Goat Gruff said he could see some beautiful rosy apples on a tree over in the field. Big Billy Goat Gruff said there was plenty of lovely clover there. And Great Big Billy Goat Gruff said he had seen ripe red berries growing there as well. They all longed to cross the river.

There was a low bridge that crossed the river between the two fields, but under it there lived a horrible troll who liked to eat goats better than anything else. So the three Billy Goats Gruff never dared to cross the bridge into the lovely empty field in case the troll caught them.

One day Little Billy Goat Gruff felt very, very hungry and he told his brothers: 'I'm going to cross over the bridge and eat some of those rosy apples.'

His brothers said, 'Be careful; remember the troll. He's certain to catch you.'

But Little Billy Goat Gruff was determined. Off he went, trit-trot, trit-trot, over the bridge. 'I'm too small for him,' he said.

When he was halfway across the bridge, the troll suddenly put his head out and said, 'Who's that running, trit-trot, trit-trot, over my bridge?'

'It's only me, Little Billy Goat Gruff.'

'I'm going to eat you up,' said the troll.

But Little Billy Goat Gruff said, 'Don't eat me, because I'm only *Little* Billy Goat Gruff. I've got a brother called *Big* Billy Goat Gruff, who is much bigger and fatter than I am. Why don't you wait for him?'

'All right,' growled the troll, 'I will.'

So Little Billy Goat Gruff trotted across the bridge to the other field and began to eat all the long green grass and the beautiful rosy apples.

Big Billy Goat Gruff saw that Little Billy Goat Gruff had got safely across; so off he went too, trit-trot, trit-trot, over the bridge.

When he was halfway across, the troll put his head out and said, 'Who's that running, trit-trot, trit-trot, over my bridge?'

'It's only Big Billy Goat Gruff.'

'Then I'm going to eat you up,' growled the troll.

But Big Billy Goat Gruff said, 'Don't eat me, because I'm only *Big* Billy Goat Gruff. I've got a brother called *Great* Big Billy Goat Gruff, who is still bigger and fatter than I am. Why don't you wait for him?'

'All right,' grunted the troll, 'I will.'

So Big Billy Goat Gruff trotted across the bridge to the other side and began to feast on the long green grass and the lovely clover.

Great Big Billy Goat Gruff thought it was time he went over to join his brothers and have some of the long green grass and the ripe red berries. So off he went, trit-trot, trit-trot, over the bridge. When he was halfway across, the troll put out his head and said, 'Who's that running, trit-trot, trit-trot, over my bridge?'

'It's Great Big Billy Goat Gruff.'

'You're the one I'm going to gobble up,' growled the troll. 'I've been waiting for you.'

Trying not to look frightened, Great Big Billy Goat Gruff said, 'Oh, have you? You just try to gobble me up and see what happens.'

Then the troll jumped up on to the bridge, but Great Big Billy Goat Gruff put down his head, ran at the troll and knocked him off the bridge and into the river. The troll disappeared howling under the water and was drowned.

Great Big Billy Goat Gruff trotted across the bridge to the other side and joined Big Billy Goat Gruff and Little Billy Goat Gruff in their new field. They all ate the long green grass, and Great Big Billy Goat Gruff ate the ripe red berries, Big Billy Goat Gruff ate the lovely clover, and Little Billy Goat Gruff ate all the beautiful rosy apples. And they all grew very fat.

The publisher gratefully acknowledges the following, for permission to reproduce copyright material in this anthology:

'The Little Wooden Horse' by Ursula Moray Williams from *Adventures of the Little Wooden Horse* first published by Harrap 1938, copyright © Ursula Moray Williams, 1938, reprinted by permission of Chambers Harrap Publishers Ltd; 'Clever Cakes' by Michael Rosen, illustrated by Caroline Holden, from *Clever Cakes and Other Stories* first published by Walker Books Ltd 1991, text copyright © Michael Rosen, 1991, reprinted by permission of Walker Books Ltd; 'The Orchestra That Lost Its Voice' by Geraldine McCaughrean from *The Treasury of Goodnight Stories* first published by Marshall Cavendish 1982, copyright © Geraldine McCaughrean, 1982, reprinted by kind permission of the author; 'Ostriches Can't Fly' by Jeremy Strong from *The Treasury of Goodnight Stories* first published by Marshall Cavendish 1982, copyright © Jeremy Strong, 1982, reprinted by kind permission of the author; *Miss Dose the Doctors' Daughter* by Allan Ahlberg first published by Viking Kestrel and in Puffin Books 1988, copyright © Allan Ahlberg, 1988, reprinted by kind permission of the author; 'Ticky Picky Boom Boom' by Pat Thomson from *A Pocketful of Stories for Five-Year-Olds* first published by Doubleday 1991, copyright © Pat Thomson, 1991, reprinted by kind permission of the author; 'A Thousand Yards of Sea' by Adèle Geras from *Cricket* magazine 1976, copyright © Adèle Geras 1976, reprinted by kind permission of the author; *Blessu* by Dick King-Smith first published by Hamish Hamilton Ltd 1990, copyright © Fox Busters Ltd, 1990, reprinted by permission of Penguin Books Ltd; 'Hedgehogs Don't Eat Hamburgers' by Vivian French from *Hedgehogs Don't Eat Hamburgers* first published in Puffin Books 1993, copyright © Vivian French, 1993, reprinted by permission of Penguin Books Ltd; 'Mrs Simkin's Bathtub' by Linda Allen from *The Puffin Children's Treasury* first published in Great Britain by Viking Kestrel 1985, copyright © Linda Allen, 1985, reprinted by kind permission of the author, c/o Rogers, Coleridge & White Ltd, 20 Powis Mews, London W11 1JN; *The Horrendous Hullabaloo* by Margaret Mahy first published by Hamish Hamilton Ltd 1992, copyright © Margaret Mahy, 1992, reprinted by permission of Penguin Books Ltd; 'Puffling in a Pickle' by Margaret Ryan from *Puffling in a Pickle* first published in Puffin Books 1995, copyright © Margaret Ryan, 1995, reprinted by permission of Penguin Books Ltd; 'Cold Feet' by Susan Eames from *More Stories from Playschool* first published by BBC Publications 1976, copyright © Susan Eames, 1972, reprinted by kind permission of the author; 'The Fish Cart' by Ruth Manning-Sanders from *Fox Tales* first published by Methuen Children's Books 1976, copyright © Ruth Manning-Sanders, 1976, reprinted by kind permission of the author; 'Wil's Tail' by Hazel Hutchins from *The Oxford Christmas Storybook* first published by Oxford University Press 1990, copyright © Hazel Hutchins, 1990, reprinted by kind permission of the author.

Every effort has been made to trace the copyright holders. The publisher would like to hear from any copyright holder not acknowledged.